MW01222423

Charades

A Novella By

Todd Foley

Cedar Rock Publishers

Copyright © 2016 Todd Foley

Published by Cedar Rock Publishers.

ISBN: 1533119880
ISBN-13: 978-1533119889

Printed in the United States of America. Registered with the Library of Congress.

Cover art by Jessica M. Cooper.

Connect with Todd on Twitter @tdiddy1234 or at Scribbledrevisions.com.

This story is entirely fictional.

ALSO BY TODD FOLEY

Eastbound Sailing (2012)

Man Speak: Conversations On Manhood, Responsibility and [not] Growing Up (2013)
[co-authored with Dave Lukas & Andrew Zahn]

Responses To *Eastbound Sailing* (via Amazon)

"Eastbound Sailing is a compact, compelling, and captivating debut novel from Todd Foley. It's a worthwhile read, and offers big payoffs for the empathetic reader."
T.W.S. Hunt, author of *Winter With God*

"A story about self-discovery and finding one's self among the chaos that life throws at us, sometimes unexpectedly. You connect with the characters, you love them, you hate them, you understand them, you even cry with them."
Ak Akkawi, journalist

"A redemptive tale of sorrow, remorse, discovery and joy viewed through its characters' different philosophical constructs." Cole Bradburn, blogger

"The story pulls you in and takes you on a journey. It makes you care about the characters and what happens to them."
Jim Woods, author of *Ready, Aim, Fire!*

"Angst, hope, and forgiveness are themes explored in a worthy manner." Brandon Clements, author of *Every Bush Is Burning*

"Foley writes like a jazz musician. This was a masterfully written story from the uncertain beginning to the unexpected ending." Tolu A.

"Chapter after chapter beckoned me to come in further. Until tears stung in my eyes and pain stabbed at my heart." Lisa T.

"Painful, raw, infuriating and strangely comforting."
Robert H.

"Foley shows understanding of human nature and his characters are real." Sherry D.

"The writing is clear, clean, and to the point, without a wasted word in telling this tale." Matt B.

Charades

=

To my daughter Abreanna, who has already made my story so rich and full. I am beyond humbled to be able to watch your story unfold every day.

"Some stories, you use up. Others use you up."
Chuck Palahnuik

=

Todd Foley

=

1

My name is Otis, and that's all you need to know for now.

What you do need to know is that I'm cold. It's early in the morning and the Skytrain isn't insulated that well. There are a few other people on the train - the same group of commuters I see each morning - but their bodies don't radiate much heat. Even if they do, we tend to keep our distance from each other. But that's okay. I can be content with the cold. My elderly frame feels cold wherever I go.

I have been walking out of the Waterfront Skytrain station at precisely 5:15 every morning for the past fifteen years. Today is no exception.

The station's marble-floor lobby is part of my daily routine. My existence.

The cold air blasts my face as I open the door of the main entrance out to the street. It's light outside, but still cold. A crisp, fall morning in Vancouver. The wind is blowing off the nearby ocean, bringing a few maple leaves that join me on my walk.

I fasten the buttons on my pea coat and place my hands in my pocket. The right pocket is filled with quarters. They're cold, but they'll be warm soon.

Two blocks south on Seymour Street at the intersection of Pender stands the next part of my morning: Antonio, a street vender who makes the best coffee in the city. Maybe not the best, but my favourite; Italians know how to brew. Perhaps what makes him my favourite is that I don't need to speak. He sees me coming, fills a paper cup with coffee, cream and raw sugar, stirs it and puts on a lid, handing me the cup in exchange for the five quarters I just fished out of my pocket. I never stop walking, and we never speak. It's a perfectly timed exchange that we've nailed down to an art.

I don't drink it yet. I let it warm my left hand.

My right hand is busy pulling two additional quarters out of my pocket. You see, there's a newspaper stand approximately twelve steps past Antonio's kiosk. Kuldeep has my copy of the *Vancouver Sun* ready. This time, I stop. I only have one hand free, so I give her the quarters, reach for the paper and tuck it under my left arm. Then, I walk on. Kuldeep and I also have a mutual understanding that we don't need to exchange words. As I said earlier, today is like any other day.

At this point, my right hand returns to the pocket with the quarters. Warm coins give me a sense of security, knowing I still have enough money for unexpected costs.

A homeless man sits on the street corner, wrapped in a blanket, holding a tin can and looking up at me. I say, "Good morning." He nods in acknowledgment. Then I walk on. This occurs every day, but I never give him any quarters.

I turn right on Dunsmuir Street. Four shops down, and I've arrived at my destination. Coastal Meats, my source of livelihood for the past fifteen years.

I finally drink my coffee in one motion. It's cool enough to consume, warm enough to comfort. I drop it in a public waste bin.

I reach into the right pocket of my jeans, pulling out a ring with three keys. One for home, one for the shop, and one for a lock box.

I look at my watch. 5:30 am. Time to open the shop. Not for business, just for prep.

With a turn of the key, the outer gate unlocks and rolls up inside the building. Now I can open the shop's entrance with the same key. I really should get a second lock made for safety purposes, but I have enough on my mind already to remember that.

A vehicle pulls up behind me. It's my food supplier. Every other morning, the company brings me my order of seafood, beef and poultry. Only seafood today.

I look at the boxes - five, to be precise - and sign the papers. He drives off, and I carry the boxes into the shop one by one. My sixty-year-old back is surprisingly strong.

The display cases stay on overnight, keeping the internal air cold enough so that the ice doesn't melt.

Before I do anything, I rotate the chicken breasts that have been marinating in a bowl since yesterday. I hope they sell by the end of the day; I'll mark them down fifty per cent by two pm if need be. People are starved for deals, and I'll still make a bit of profit.

I turn on the soft rock radio station.

Time to put today's shipment on the ice. I open up the first four boxes. They're filled with shellfish - scallops, mussels, clams and oysters - all caught in the greater Vancouver area. They smell like the ocean, sand wedged between the cracks of the shells. Most people cringe when the see sand in their shellfish or dirt on their produce. Dirtiness is a sign of purity. Nevertheless, I should clean these critters before they go on the ice. Appearance is important to my customers.

One box at a time, I place the shellfish in the sink and rinse them under cold water. Once the sand is gone, they go in a large colander. Same process with the next three boxes.

Box number five contains my favourite catch: salmon. I put one whole fish directly on the ice. I gut the second, cutting it into three small fillets. Some people like the ready-made product, while the more primitive prefer doing it themselves. I find myself somewhere in the middle. Depends on the day.

I hear a knock. I turn. I see a young man outside the shop looking in. I recognize him. It's Garret, a server at a cafe just down the street. Garret works at this cafe to cover his tuition at Emily Carr University, and occasionally works extra hours doing prep work in the morning.

After washing my hands, I open the front door and then lock it again once he's in. His thick-rimmed glasses fog up right away.

"Morning, Otis," he says. Today, Garret is wearing dark brown corduroy pants, a grey cardigan and a red scarf. He wears the same sort of outfit each day, shopping at Value Village over any high-end store along Robson Street. The only time he frequents that part of the city is to take part in the Occupy Vancouver protests outside the art gallery.

"Hi, Garret."

Garret tells me that the cafe needs five pounds of marinated chicken for their lunch special. Too bad he didn't get the marked down the price later on. But I give him the discount anyway. He's a good kid. I admire his ethic.

"Getting ready for school?" I ask.

"Yes, and no," he responds. "I have some paintings I've been working on. More for pleasure, though. It helps to keep practicing."

"I see." I often see his paintings on display in the cafe window. Signed, with a small photo next to the canvas. He's gifted.

He writes me a cheque, and off he goes.

I go back to the clean seafood in the sink, lift the colander and shake off the excess water. Too much water will cause the shells to freeze to the ice. That happened before when trying to get them for a customer. It was embarrassing. It hasn't again since. I consider myself methodical and am careful to avoid the repetition of mistakes, especially in front of others.

With the seafood on the ice, I break down the cardboard boxes and put them next to the back door, which opens up to an alley. The recycling truck comes on Wednesday mornings. It's Tuesday, and the stack of cardboard is quite large. I'll have to give myself enough time to get everything outside tomorrow morning. I may be strong, but I move slowly.

I notice a few spots of water on the concrete floor. Probably from transferring the seafood over to the ice. It will put off a foul odor; I really should mop that up before anyone gets here.

The mop and bucket sit next to the sink, placed there for convenience. I fill the bucket, add a splash of bleach, dip the mop, ring out the excess water and clean up the mess.

I hear a familiar song on the radio. "Drift Away" by Clarence Carter. The mess is cleaned up but I keep mopping to the rhythm. I move slowly, but intentionally. I let my mind go blank. Still mopping. Sometimes just existing in the present without worrying about the next phase is a necessity.

I look at the clock. 6:30 am. Time passes quickly when you block out the world. But my mind is refreshed, and the floor is clean.

I place the "Open" sign in the window. Customers should come shortly.

The morning goes by in a flash most days and calms down around lunch time. I'll usually close for fifteen minutes, walk over to Tim Hortons and bring back a cup of chili. I eat it while reading the newspaper. That's what I did today. It isn't an exciting meal, but I enjoy it every time. Even in the warm summer months.

At this point in my life, it's too much work to pass judgment on issues or people, let alone food. I spend my energy getting to work and living in observation. Nothing is ever what it seems at the surface, and people are far more complex than they let on. Even I am. Most people are consumed by covering their imperfections with masks of normality. I suppose I wear one as well. Sometimes.

The afternoon hours go by at a slower pace. Customers stop in to pick up ingredients for dinner, usually tired from their day's work. I'm tired as well. That means it was a profitable day, though, so I welcome such exhaustion.

I start my closing routine by balancing the till. My bank is still open after I close, so I can drop off my cash on the way home. A nice convenience. I place the envelope on the counter for now.

Next, I mop the floor. This time, I'm eager to go home, so I make sure not to lose myself in the music again. But I leave the radio on. A soundtrack is always welcomed. I feel less alone.

The mopping wasn't too intense today. I clean out the bucket, rinse out the mop and place them both back by the sink. I always keep things where they're supposed to be, nothing is ever achieved without strict attention to detail. For me, it's all in the details.

I turn off the radio, dim the lights and walk out the front door after placing the cash envelope in my pocket. I pull the gate down after locking the door, then I lock the gate. My bank is one block in the other direction. Very kind folks in there. Today, though, I use the outside ATM to deposit the cash. I have a few things I need to get done around the house when I get home. This way is more efficient.

And then I'm off, heading north toward the Skytrain station. The sun radiates on my left side. I feel warm. On that side, at least. My right side is still cold.

I pass the homeless man again. We make eye contact, and I nod in acknowledgement. I can tell that he's cold, but I continue walking.

Suddenly I feel guilty for focusing on my right-side pocket. He's a man of great potential in a dire circumstance; I am a man of privilege, blessed with the security of my routine. I long to use that security for the greater good. Just not today. Not yet.

I enter the vast lobby of the Waterfront station, scan my pass and take the escalator down to the train platform. I board soon after.

My name is Otis, and this is my life's work.

2

Everyone has at least one vice. Something to which they constantly need access or within close proximity. A sense of security. An extension of their identity. A habit they can't break.

What's yours?

Mine is hand sanitizer.

There are three dispensers in the shop. One by the cash register, one on top of the glass display case and one by the front entrance for customers - plus the travel-size bottle in my coat pocket. I keep an extra liter of sanitizer in the back of the shop for whenever I need to refill one of the dispensers. Interestingly, the one by the entrance rarely gets depleted. I guess customers aren't as paranoid of germs as I am. As I said, though, this is *my* vice.

It isn't just for my own benefit. I sanitize for my patrons' protection. You have no idea just how dangerous it is to step foot inside a meat shop. Opportunities for cross-contamination abound; that's where my vice comes in to save the day.

Life-threatening dangers lurk around every corner of our lives, often where we live out the monotonous moments of the day. Crossing the street. Driving a car. Buying uncooked meat. Yet there's some force that, most days, prevents these calamities from occurring. The cell phone that rings before you step off the sidewalk without looking both ways. The red light that stops you from the accident that would have happened on the other side of the intersection. The butcher who sanitizes his hands between wiping his nose and wrapping your salmon fillet.

It's funny, though, when you think about it. No one even knows that they're being saved, or that they need saving at all. Oh, but they do.

That's why I always keep my sanitizer within reach. Each time I use it, it's a ritual of sorts. A cleansing, paving the way forward with purity. Forgive and forget the past.

Maybe I use this illustration too loosely. Am I merely trying to cover my tracks? I guess that's why they call it a vice: it's generally considered to be slightly depraved.

I think I know what Will's vice is.

Will is one of my most favourite patrons. He's a pastor at a church in the downtown area and rents a West End studio apartment. Beautiful view, but a humble residence. His car, a beat up Rabbit, helps get this point across. I'll confess that I've never been to a service. He's invited me a couple times, but never forcefully. I appreciate that.

I noticed something when he came into the shop yesterday. He was wearing dark jeans, a blazer and a Mumford & Sons t-shirt. He looked fatigued.

"Why so tired, Will?" I asked.

"Oh, you know," he said. "A busy week meeting with people from the congregation."

"Problems?"

"None with the church. Just catching up with people one-on-one."

"Regular meetings?"

"Some regular, some spontaneous." He put his hands in his pockets. "Everyone has something going on in their life. Sometimes they just need a listening ear, and I try to be that for them."

I nod in agreement. A very noble man.

Will ordered three cuts of chicken breasts marinated in honey, garlic, ginger and green onion. Today's special. Seemed to be a lot for one person.

"Talking with people must work up an appetite," I said with a slight smile.

Will laughed, then explained: one cut for dinner, one for a second helping and one for lunch after church the next day. He plans ahead. I admire that.

As I wrapped up the meat, a couple other customers walked in. A mother and her son, I assumed.

"Pastor Will!" the boy exclaimed.

Will turned, smiled and returned the greeting to the boy. He offered a strong high-five and asked how his week has been. I wrapped Will's chicken and - after sanitizing - rang up the mother for a pound of ground beef. She used the sanitizer after putting her credit card back in her purse. I smiled to myself.

The boy - must be in high school - asked Will if he could get together for coffee sometime this next week. I'm not sure if it was for a serious issue or just to catch up. Either way, this isn't my business. I tell myself that, yet I still listened with interest.

Without missing a beat, Will offered to pick him up next Tuesday evening at seven.

Will smiled as the mother and son left. Then he let out a sigh, struggling to maintain his smile.

"Never a quiet moment, Otis," he said. "That's why I shop for things ahead of time."

He gave me his credit card, entered his PIN and took the card back along with the receipt.

"Thanks for helping me keep up the pace," he said, smiling as he picked up the chicken and turned to leave.

I nodded and gave him a slow wave goodbye with my right hand. The meetings, the people, they never seem to get the best of him. Somehow, he keeps up the energy.

That's when I saw it: Will's vice is his smile.

Maybe Will and I are both crippled by our vices. Maybe this crippling is necessary. After all, they keep us going. He looked like he could use a break, though. The heart can only pour out so much love before something fractures.

I look at my clock. Time for lunch. I sanitize my hands again.

3

It's been a busy week, and I'm tired. I could use a break from the shop. I just need to get out for a bit. I've been here long enough for people to know that I'm coming back; I never leave my base unattended for long.

I switch the sign to "Closed," turn out the lights and then lock up, walking to the Tim Hortons a few blocks away. The fresh air provides instant relief. The tension in my neck subsides. My eyelids are less heavy. I smile. Oh, how good it feels to smile.

Don't get me wrong. This shop is my life's work; I love serving the community with the best meats available, and I enjoy the chance to get to know my customers. They are beautiful people. They really are.

I love waking up each morning and riding the Skytrain and seeing other people start their day. The city comes alive when everyone shows up. The people are the city's oxygen; without us, it would be a metropolitan wasteland of glass and concrete. A waste, indeed!

But even a lover of routine like myself can become fatigued. Not so much from work, but from bad news.

There's so much bad news every day, and I always hear it. In the papers, on the radio, on these very streets. Sometimes even in my shop. I could share these stories with you. Maybe I will, someday. Someone else needs to hear these stories, because they can be too much for me to bear. But I respect people's dignity, so for that reason, I'll keep their stories to myself for now.

Have you ever driven by an accident on the side of the road? Your stomach turns, your breathing stills and you're suddenly aware of life's fragility, offering a quick "thank you" to the universe that you somehow were spared. However, you can't look away from the wreck; you need to know what happened.

Despite how hard it is to hear all the bad news, I can't turn away from it. I have to stay on top of things. I need to know what's going on in the world around me. If I can't take any immediate action towards solving these problems, I at least can pray. Most days, that's all I can do as I watch and listen.

That's why I brought today's paper with me. After ordering my regular chili combo, I sit at a table by the window; it's nice being able to see outside. I search through the pages, trying to find some ray of hope. All I see are stories of war, crime and scandal. A gang shooting in the city. A double homicide down in Washington. Another terrorist attack overseas. A politician's dirty laundry being hung out in the open. A dip in the stock market, prompting analysts to to predict another sweep of job cuts - cuts which bring a surge of

additional bad news for each former employee,
especially those with a family and a mortgage.
Some days, my heart just aches.

I have to turn away for a moment. When I look up, my
eyes catch a homeless man sitting on the sidewalk
outside, leaning up against a rusted green newspaper
box. That's unfair, actually; his clothes are dirty and he
looks like he hasn't showered in a few days, but he may
not be homeless. I hate it when people jump to
conclusions, and I know I'm guilty of this as well.
Everyone is so much more than they appear.

I wonder what this man's story is. Maybe he has some
good news he can share with me.

I see him turn, looking toward an officer - security,
perhaps - approaching him. The officer is saying
something I can't hear because of the glass that separates
me from these two men. The man starts motioning with
his hands, appearing agitated, explaining something to
the officer. The officer looks like he's yelling, pointing
down the road so as to direct the man's attention
elsewhere. I can't tell what's going on, but they seem to
be arguing now. Whatever they're talking about, it
doesn't look pleasant.

The officer takes out his walkie-talkie, turns to the side
and starts talking into the device. The man on the
sidewalk is still yelling, but the officer doesn't pay him
any attention. Finally, the man stands up, says something
else and walks away, raising his hand in the air and
giving the officer the middle finger. Whatever
transpired, it didn't end well. More bad news. Again,
I'm saddened.

I then turn to the counter in the restaurant, looking at the woman working the cash register. She must be in her thirties, but it's hard to tell. She's looking down at her phone, reading a text message, I assume. She smiles. I wonder what the message says. A note from a friend, her mother or father, her child, her boyfriend - or girlfriend? A quick "hello," a question, a response to an earlier question, an invitation to go somewhere or just a funny story, perhaps?

Then I wonder: What is *her* story? What's her home like? What are her dreams? What are her regrets? What brings her joy? What paralyzes her with fear?

I notice the clock behind me. Half an hour has gone by already. Time to get back to the shop. I wish I could know these answers. Maybe I could help. Contemplation provides a nice escape from reality.

Whoever this woman is, and whatever her circumstances, she's smiling. That can only mean she just received some good news in one form or another. God knows we all could use a little more of that.

4

I've said that I take pride in knowing the details and managing everything myself. That was true, for the most part. I lied about one thing. Not so much lied, but I withheld some information. That's different from a lie, right?

Either way, here's the truth: I'm too old to handle my finances. A personal bank account is one thing; the books of an established business is another. I only ask for help when I know I really need it.

That's where I'm headed today. To meet with Andre, my personal accountant. He is a senior partner at a firm just a few blocks away and often works evenings, which fits my needs as I can go see him after my shop closes. As well, Andre comes by every Thursday after work to get a sirloin steak. He has his rituals, just like me.

We're meeting today to go over the quarterly report Andre prepared based off of September through November; he uses these findings to give projections and recommendations for the winter quarter. I already have a follow-up appointment for the end of February to see how it turned out, but he's always correct.

Andre works in a beautiful high rise, twenty-two floors tall. The accounting firm shares the building with several other companies. I'm guessing there's a lavish penthouse suite on the top floor, overlooking the entire city with panoramic views of the surrounding ocean and mountains. I like to live simply, but I'd be lying if I said I didn't sometimes covet a home like that. That would be two lies in one day.

I take the elevator up to the eighteenth floor. Once I step out of the retractable doors, I see signs for every business but the one I want. I step back in, press the number seventeen, and then step out once I'm down one floor. That has never happened. I don't make mistakes.

The firm's waiting area has a sleek, minimalist design. Black walls, black tile floors and white trim along the door frames. A few tall glass vases with white lilies. Simple. Beautiful.

"Can I help you, sir?"

I turn to the welcome desk on my right and see a young receptionist wearing a blue tooth device in her ear. She's new.

"I'm here to see Andre," I explain.

"Oh, yes. Otis, correct?"

"Yes."

"Right on time. I'll let him know you're here."

"Thank you."

She walks away to tell Andre that I've arrived, then comes back to her desk. I remain standing.

"We meet again, Otis," I hear from behind me.

I look up and see my accountant. He's dressed in his usual business suit, his Middle Eastern features framed by a strong jawline, a shaved head and a dark soul patch below his lower lip. His strongest fashion statement, though, is his confidence.

I turn and follow Andre into his corner office. He has a beautiful view of Coal Harbor, luxury yachts, the trees of Stanley Park and high-end condos.

"How've you been keeping?" Andre asks as he walks over to a filing cabinet. I see that he has a small, red line on the back of his head. Must have cut himself shaving this morning.

"Well," I say. "Eager to hear your thoughts."

"You're doing alright, Otis," he says, turning around and sitting down in his chair on the other side of the dark wood desk. "Pretty good numbers this past quarter. However, I'd consider cutting your prices for a week in December."

Cutting prices? How can that be profitable?

"Don't I already have low enough costs compared to other meat shops?"

"Your prices are good, but this actually could be setting you up for success," Andre says.

"How?"

"You slash your prices for the week - call it your 'blowout sale' or whatever you'd like - and try to really move more sales. You can even run an ad in one of the free community papers. Give good deals for Christmas, that kind of deal. Discounts will expand your customer base. Then, you raise them up again once you've attained new clientele. That adds value to your product."

I'm confused.

"Don't I already have value?" I ask.

"You do," Andre explains, "but your sales haven't really been matching your orders. At least not as much as they should. You're not selling everything that you order. Most, but not all. I know you sometimes freeze the old meats and use them at home, but every piece of meat you don't sell, you're basically bleeding money out of your ass."

I cringe. Andre never was one to shy away from profanity. I don't find it very professional, but I can't find a better accountant. I make sacrifices when I need to.

"I don't like waste," he says. "Not on my watch."

"Well, let's try it," I say. "You haven't steered me wrong once."

"I always deliver, Otis. Always have, always will."

Andre walks me to the elevator.

"You have anything else planned for the evening?" he asks.

"Just punching the right number in the elevator," I say with a laugh.

"Go to the wrong floor?"

"Eighteen, accidentally."

Andre cringes.

"I never go to that floor," he says.

"Why?"

"My parents' old apartment number in the suburbs. Maybe they still live there. Beats the hell out of me." He walks back to his office, waving me goodbye as he stares off.

I stand as the elevator doors close, puzzled.

5

I hear all the time that Wednesday is the most depressing day of the week. Two days of labour gone by, two more to trudge through still. When all is said and done, half is just the incomplete state of what will be.

The shop has been busy today, though, and it's only quarter past eight. Life is happening here at that halfway mark.

The door opens loudly, and before I turn to see her face, I know that it's Sheila. She's at the display case already, looking at her phone. As always, her appearance is as loud as her entrance. She is wearing a lime green hoodie and Lululemon yoga pants, and her Coach bag is bigger than the box of steaks that was delivered today. That's a slight exaggeration, but this is Sheila. Her long, fire-red hair - not natural - is up in a bun right on top of her head; it looks like a beehive. Her makeup is bold, and her large black sunglasses - on an overcast day - hide most of her face aside from her broad smile. It isn't so much a warm

smile, but rather a statement to everyone in the room that
Sheila has arrived.

"Good morning, Sheila," I manage.

She looks up, smiling insincerely. "Sweetie," she says.
"Hi."

"Making the rounds?"

"Always. Kids are off to school and I've got the world to
conquer before I pick them up," she says.

"What brings you downtown this early?" I ask. Sheila's
family lives in Kerisale, about twenty-eight minutes
outside the downtown core. I know because she told me
once. I admire precision.

"You're the only butcher who isn't useless and
incompetent, Otis," she says with a laugh as she pulls
her sunglasses up over the top of her head. "I'm afraid
I've become known as the wicked bitch of Kerisdale."

"I try to make people happy," I say. I really mean it, too.
"What will it be today?"

"Eight pork chops, boneless, trimmed of all fat." She
emphasizes the last four words. Her reputation has been
earned from seeing those demands met. I believe in
customer retention, so I get to work.

"How is it already this late in the year?" Sheila asks,
clicking her pen as she talks. She does this a lot. "The
kids are nailing their classes, like always. Of course
there would be hell to pay at home if it was otherwise.

Not from their father, from me. He's too busy slaying it at work to monitor them at home."
Sheila's husband is an esteemed civil lawyer at a law firm in the city, representing the interests of environmentalist groups. From what I hear, he always wins his cases. Vancouver is the place for pro-nature groups, and he makes sure nature gets the last word over big oil companies. How he ended up with a wife like Sheila, I don't know, but confidence must attract confidence.

She has now clicked her pen eighteen times, watching my every move as I trim each chop of all the fat and wrap each piece in cling wrap. She doesn't break her stare or acknowledge the pen.

"My husband is nearing the close a big case today," she says. "So this celebratory dinner has to be perfect. You're the only person I trust to not screw up the ingredients, Otis." She smiles as she says this, but I hear the threat in her voice; she wants me to hear it. "After this, it's off to get my hair and nails done before lunch, then cleaning and cooking. Let me tell you, it's a full-time job running a family."

"You learn the ropes from your mother?" I ask.

"Sadly no," she says. "My parents died in a car accident when I was young."

"I'm sorry to hear that," I say as I place all the meat in an insulated bag along with a scoop of ice in case Sheila is out for a while. "Loss is always hard."

"I've learned to become every woman. What do I owe you?"

I run it through the till. "Twenty-two even," I say.

She has a cheque ready, writes in the amount, clicks her pen six times as she reads it over and then hands it to me. I give her the bag in return, along with a receipt.

"Thank you for never letting me down, Otis. It's time for the queen to set sail," she says as she pulls her sunglasses down over her eyes.

6

Easter and Christmas. Like many people I know, these are the two days of the year I go to church. It's nothing against the church or its people, or even the condition of my own soul. I actually love the idea of church, and I'm inspired and challenged by its teachings. I want to be a better person. I love the idea of relying on a power greater than me. When it all comes down to it, though, I simply don't have the time to show up like I should.

Here's the crazy part: today I am walking towards a church, and it isn't Easter or Christmas.

This is Will's congregation. I haven't been to this one before. He invites me to services most every instance he comes to my store. Finally, I'm here. An evening service made it easier for me to attend.

It's an evangelical free church. Honestly, I don't really know what that phrase means. I believe the word "evangelical" has a more loaded meaning south of the border. I always took it to mean "typical Christian." Not in a negative way at all, but belief in the basics: be born again, attend church, get baptized, don't swear, abstain until marriage, minimize intake of alcohol and generally strive to set a positive example to others. I admire all of these traits, and I presume that the congregants inside Will's church try to hold to them. I hope I won't feel too much of an outsider.

I open the main entrance door and am greeted by a gentleman. He gives a sincere smile and a strong hand shake. "Welcome," he says. "Is this your first time with us?"

"Yes," I answer without hesitation.

He smiles again. "It's so great having you here today. Welcome." I believe him. I smile back.

The foyer is bright. There are two tables to the right, each one being used to display pamphlets and brochures which outline different programs that the church offers. I don't look at them. I imagine that they're admirable, but like I said, I'm busy enough with work. The fact that I'm here on a Sunday is enough of a miracle.

I think that the service has already started because the doors to the main auditorium are closed. I open them and see that the music has stopped and the attendees are siting down. I find a spot near the back.

Will has now taken the stage. He's dressed in his usual attire. Dark jeans, a blazer and a grey shirt. Casual, but he still looks sharp. His eyes still have dark circles under them.

"Today," he begins, "we're talking about serving one another. It's so easy to serve when we're free of distraction, and when our ducks are all in a row. Here's the thing: it should be our primary act of extending the love of God to the world around us."

I feel as though I'm meant to hear this sermon.

Will then begins his message about the Good Samaritan. I know of the common phrase used in mainstream culture, but I never knew its origins until today.

A Jewish man was on a journey and was robbed, beaten and abandoned on the side of the road. A priest walks by, sees the Jew, but continues walking. A Levite walks by after, and he too passes by. Finally, a third man from Samaria walks by. Samaritans are despised by Jews, but he stops and gives aid to the wounded man. He defied cultural expectations and chose to serve. This, Will says, is one of Jesus' greatest and most important teachings.

Suddenly, it all makes sense, and I fully understand why Will loves to serve - especially at the drop of a hat. It's his love language, and it's his way of bringing God's kingdom to Earth, like he just said. This is the fuel behind his strained smiles.

The sermon ends, and the musicians come back up to lead a couple more songs. Most people sing with their eyes closed. I don't know the lyrics or melodies, so I just listen.

The lead singer then dismisses everyone. The attendees stand up slowly and make their way out. As I come to the foyer, I see that Will has already made his way to the front door, greeting everyone as they leave. I stand here and watch. It's so evident, Will's love for these people. He's easy to talk to, and he genuinely cares. When people say that they could use a one-on-one talk to discuss something serious, Will says, "Yes, I will make it work." He has now said this to at least six people since I've been watching.

I finally walk outside. It's dark, and it's foggy. When Will sees the fog, his eyes widen, and his face goes white, like he has seen a ghost. He walks back inside.

7

You're probably sick of hearing about my routine. Honestly, some days I crave something different. So today, I decided to stir things up a bit. I'm taking my lunch break at a new restaurant.

I choose The Venti, the cafe where Garret works. A reclaimed industrial building, the exterior is nothing remarkable, other than the business' name in a deep red cursive font against a black backdrop. Inside, the feel is minimalist with a few strong accent colors here and there. Five tables, and a bar near the back. The name refers to the fact that they only make twenty-ounce beverages.

Garret is currently serving a couple at their table, and he looks up and sees me. We both nod. He walks over to me.

"Well, look who finally decided to check it out," he says, smiling slightly.

"I was in the mood for something different today," I tell him.

"Sit anywhere you'd like, Otis."

I choose a two-person table near the entrance, which offers some fresh air when the door opens and a full view of the cafe.

Garret brings me a menu, a one-page sheet that lists two salads, three sandwiches, a soup and a dessert. The menu changes daily, Garret tells me. I choose a bowl of chili. I may be switching up my routine, but I can only be so daring.

About ten minutes later, Garret brings me my order. It looks hearty. I am now the only customer, so he joins me at the table.

"Garret," I say, "I seem to recall you saying you hate this part of the city. Do you live in the area?"

"I do hate it here," he says. "Rich privileged pricks who think they own everything and everyone. But Vancouver ain't cheap, and rich pricks' tips help pay the rent."

"Did you grow up around here?"

"No, over by Point Grey."

I know this area. Point Grey is one of the most expensive postal codes in Canada.

"Do your parents still live there?" I ask.

"Yeah. They were both born into a lot of money, second generation doctors, teach at the university here. My brothers followed suit. Working every hour to pay for shit they don't even get to enjoy. I couldn't wait to break out."

I sense his residual angst.

"You must commute a bit, then?" I ask, just before taking the first spoonful of my chili. It's okay, but a bit too spicy.

"About ten minutes east on the Skytrain. I live over on Commercial Drive in a crappy apartment with two other guys. One of them makes burritos at a food joint there - he's in line to take over the place some day - and the other guy works construction and busks on the weekends."

"Busks?" I'm not familiar with that term.

"Playing music on the street for tips. He plays the harmonica like a god. None of us make tons of cash through our passion projects, but it keeps us alive."

Keeps us alive. Good on them for feeding their passions. I'm inspired.

Two twenty-something men walk in through the entrance, making their way up to the bar. They're both wearing suits. Expensive ones.

"Speaking of which, I'd better make sure I don't get fired so I can keep feeding that passion project," Garret says with a smile. "Good seeing you here, Otis."

"The pleasure is all mine, Garret," I say as he walks toward the bar.

I watch Garret greet the customers, brightly engaged as he tells them the specials and schmoozes them each into trying the featured espresso drink. He's good at what he does, and he appears to care about the customers' experience.

But he seems to have a thirst for something else. Fame? Glory? Credit?

Something about Garret just doesn't seem entirely right. In all honesty, it hasn't since that Friday afternoon a couple years ago. The day I saw the *real* Garret.

But there's no time for that story right now. My lunch break is almost over. I quickly eat the rest of my chili and leave enough cash to cover the tip. I don't want to appear stingy compared to the regular patrons. That would make me stand out, and I need to blend in.

8

It has been two months since my last financial review with Andre. I followed his recommendations, and I believe they resulted in positive change. I'm not throwing food away, and I rarely take anything home with me. We'll see how it really went, though; I have a tinge of anxiety as I wait for the news.

I arrive at the firm ten minutes before my scheduled appointment. I generally budget for every minute in the day, and when I'm meeting someone, I always allow for a little buffer time. It keeps me from looking irresponsible.

My clothes are wet from the rain. I get off the elevator and let the receptionist know I'm here. I then walk to the waiting area and see the back of a woman's head as she's sitting with her back toward me. Her hair is fire red, and I immediately know who it belongs to.

"Well hello, stranger," I say as Sheila turns her head to me. She's wearing her sunglasses and scanning through her iPhone's calendar app, making notes.

"Otis!" she exclaims. "Fancy seeing you here!"

She's in her usual high-fashion yoga wear; even at a prestigious firm, Sheila calls the shots for what's appropriate.

"Shouldn't you be working on the order I left for you?" she asks.

I panic and feel my face turn pale as my forehead perspires. Sheila called? When? How did I miss it?

"Fooled you, did I?" she says with a grin.

I force a smile as my heart rate slows.

"What brings you here?" I ask.

"Meeting with my financial advisor. Retirement plans, debt repayment schedule, college funds according to projected tuition hikes for each school."

"Aren't your children still young?" I ask.

"You can never start planning too early, Otis."

Sheila and I share more common ground than I assumed.

"And what are you here for?" she asks.

"Meeting with Andre, my accountant."

Her eyes widen.

"Oh, Andre."

"You work with him too?"
"No, he's just *very* easy on the eyes."

Carnality. Therein lies our difference.

"Otis, my man," I hear Andre say as he comes around the corner. "How are we doing today?"

Sheila grins as she scans his figure. I blush on her behalf.

I greet Andre and follow him to his office.

"Let's cut right to it, Otis," he says as he sits in his chair. "Numbers look great. You're up from this time last year, and you're headed to the next quarter very strong."

I'm instantly relieved. "Thank you, Andre. I owe this all to you."

He leans back in his chair and puts his hands behind his head. "I'd tell you that failure isn't in my blood, but that wouldn't be entirely honest. I just made sure it stopped with me."

I don't follow.

"I beg your pardon?"

"Here's a little secret, Otis." He leans forward and rests his arms on the desk. "I wasn't born into success. I made it, and I made it out of nothing."

I was not expecting this, so I nod for him to go on.

"I was born in Lebanon, and my family immigrated to Vancouver when I was a kid. We came over as war refugees. Couldn't afford to live in the city, so we moved out to Surrey. It was crazy how an hour east makes such a difference in rent."

"It's true," I say, taking in Andre's story. "I don't live downtown either, it's too much for me."

"Thing is," he says, hardly acknowledging what I just said, "I grew up in a shit hole apartment. Ugly, gross and pathetic. Suite number eighteen on the third floor, no elevator. I hated that place, and I was always ashamed to call it home. As soon as I finished high school, I left. My grades were high enough that I got every scholarship I could, worked evenings at this place as a janitor, finished university at the top of my class and got hired here as a junior associate. They saw my drive and my work ethic, and now I'm a senior partner."

My eyes have widened in amazement. I had no idea Andre came from that background. Appearances can be deceiving.

"That's inspiring," I say. It's true, I am sincerely inspired by the man in front of me. But he seems incomplete.

"No way in hell was I going to stay there. I left the bottom and never looked back. Why would I, when I've got all this to show?" He spreads his arms out and looks around his office.

I follow his eyes, noting his degrees and accolades. No photos of any loved ones.

"Yes, this is indeed significant," I say.

"Now you know why I get such a high off my ideas working, because they always work. I'll never disappoint you, Otis. So long as you keep paying your invoices!" he says with a laugh.

I offer a nervous chuckle. "That would make things difficult if I didn't."

"Well, looks like we're good to go for now. We'll meet again in two months. Have Karen schedule an appointment on your way out." He stands up and shakes my hand with a strong grip. "Pleasure bringing you success, Otis."

I smile, nod and bid him goodbye.

I schedule my appointment with Karen; it's good to know her name now. I should have asked the last time I was here.

Sheila is no longer in the waiting area. I still smell her perfume.

I take the elevator down. As it's descending, I feel my heart drop a bit. How sad Andre must be. Yes, his ambition and success are to be admired, especially considering his humble background, but to be driven by shame and nothing more? I can't imagine how exhausting and lifeless that must be. I wish there was some way I could shed some perspective. Maybe I can. If I can, I really should.

9

I get anxious when I see the sunset. I probably could
have accomplished more by the end of the day, and I
stress thinking that I have to get it done tomorrow on top
of everything else I have planned. Then I remember that
someone else's busy day will start soon as mine ends,
and I talk myself down so that I can get the rest I need.
Before I know it, it'll be time to start up again. Tonight,
I choose to enjoy my walk after work.

I sometimes stop by the public library on my way home.
It's a bit out of my way, but it's a sight to be held.
Modeled after the Colosseum, I feel like I've been
transported to a simpler time. Well, not simple; it was a
venue for watching humans kill each other for sport.
Learning is a much more admirable activity.

As I make my way through the grand entrance, I see a
familiar face at a table. It's Marla. Oh, what a lovely
woman she is. The daughter of an Italian mother and an
English father, her subtle features framed by dark,
naturally wavy hair and speckled with light freckles.

"Good afternoon, dear," I say, standing about two feet away from her table.

Marla looks up from her pile of psychology and medical books and flashes a bright, genuine smile. "Otis! How are you?"

Marla is a registered nurse who rents a small apartment in the downtown east side - the poorest postal code in Canada - and shares it with a friend. With such low living expenses and a nurse's income, she donates the majority of her money to fund medical research at the University of British Columbia right here in the city. She lives simply and loves greatly. I know it's cliché, but if I had a daughter, I imagine she'd be like Marla. I hope I'd raise a woman half as strong as she is.

"Don't you spend enough time practicing medicine to not have to read all this?" I ask with a smile, pointing at all the text books.

"Just trying to stay one step ahead of death," she says. "The world could use a little less of it, don't you think?"

I admire Marla's passion for life and her desire to make it endure.

"Why don't you at least face a window? The sunset is stunning." Even though they make me anxious, I know they're soothing for most people.

"I don't like the mountains," she says, averting her eyes a bit. "I'm just not much of a nature girl, I guess."

"Never liked it?"

"I feel like they're always watching me. Silly superstition, I know."

She smirks, but it doesn't seem authentic. I wonder why. I move to a different subject.

"Haven't seen you in the shop much," I observe.

"Well, it's getting colder outside, and people do desperate things to stay warm. You could say that street nurses are in high demand right now."

"Shouldn't you be saving lives instead of reading, then?"

Marla folds her hands and places them on the text books.

"You can't fix what you don't understand, Otis."

At times I hear or read something and think to myself, *'I wish I had thought of that.'* This happens a lot when I talk to Marla.

"You still go to Union Gospel Mission at all?" I ask. UGM serves three hot meals each day to those in the community. Marla often volunteers at the organization, helping with meal preparations.

"I do when I can, but I wish I could do more."

"Do they ever take food donations? I could offer some meat. I get a great deal from my supplier."

Marla's eyes light up. "You know, they do a big Easter dinner each year for the community. How about I follow up with them and then come by your shop? I need some good cuts for myself, and I'm overdue for a proper visit."

Marla loves chicken breasts, boneless but with the skin still on. She knows how you can't achieve the same flavour without skin.

"That sounds great. I'll let you get back to work, I know your free time is valuable." I smile and give her a slight squeeze on the shoulder. She puts her hand on mine and looks me in the eye.

"You're a sweetheart, Otis. It honestly was such a treat to see you today."

"Likewise," I say.

My heart feels warm as I walk over to the new release section.

10

I remember that moment like it was five minutes ago.
Which says a lot, considering my age.

Late September, 2011. I got off the Skytrain station at
Granville Street. After walking a few blocks, I saw the
crowd. Thousands, all gathered around the Vancouver
Art Gallery. It was a protest, but a surprisingly tame one.
This is Canada, after all, the land of "please" and "thank
you," but it's the city that inspired a movement. A
Vancouver-based anti-consumerism magazine published
an article called "Occupy Wall Street," a protest against
the financial institutions. The first rally started in New
York and the spark spread across the continent. I thought
I'd come see what it was all about.

The people had every right to be angry. They lost their
jobs, homes and pursuit of happiness. Tighter
regulations kept the financial crisis at bay in Canada, but
these people here today were crying out on behalf of
their oppressed neighbours south of the border.

I see the nobility in this movement. Active citizens advocating for their fellow man, demanding justice for institutional crimes.

That's when it happened. I noticed a young man shouting on the gallery stairs. It was Garrett.

I was actually impressed by Garret's conviction and passion. I thought back to some of his art pieces, clearly inspired by justice and the battle against inequality.

I watched as Garret walked down from the steps and moved near the perimeter to a nearby cafe for food. He walked toward me, and we made eye contact.

"And here I always thought you were the quiet type, Garret," I said with a genuine smile.

"Just doing my job, Otis," he said.

"And that is?" I asked.

"Casting a light on the greatest evils of our time."

This may be my age speaking, but I couldn't help feeling annoyed at Garret's naivete. Naive. Righteous anger, but naive. That may be harsh, but it was true.

"You don't blame people for getting in over their heads?" I prodded. "Living beyond their means?"

"Even still, we're the innocent pawns who got trapped in a cruel game of chess."

"Innocent?"

Garret's friendly demeanor faded and was replaced by a stern expression.

"Oh, yes," he said, and I hear the ominous threat in his voice. "And we're taking back the board and taking out the king. I'm going to be there when we all yell 'Checkmate.'"

He put his hand on my shoulder and gave a firm squeeze. Friendly gesture aside, I felt sick to my stomach.

11

I've been down for two days. Stomach bug. Past the point of being contagious, but I still have no appetite. Working in a meat shop in a nauseous state is torture.

The smells of salmon, chicken, pork, beef and lamb overwhelm me. I always use latex gloves when I handle meat, but even the soft texture nearly puts me over the edge. I breathe in through my mouth so I can't smell it.

It almost helps, though, that today is a very busy day with customers. I'm working too fast to focus on how I feel. When the rush finally slows, the nausea returns. I immediately switch the sign to "Closed" and go for outside for my break.

It's raining so heavily today, and while I have my umbrella, I've worn mesh shoes. Mesh should be banned in Vancouver. It's an open invitation for all the cold water on the street to take up permanent residence with your feet.

I see Homeless Man taking shelter under an awning in the alley. I really should find out what his actual name is, because "Homeless Man" robs him of his dignity. He's been around here for years and we always nod "hello," but never speak. I still have a few quarters in my pocket, but keep them to myself. I can't break that tradition now.

I wonder what his story is. Who he was before he came to live here. What his life was like.

"Beautiful day today, eh?" I ask. It's a shallow and predictable way to engage someone, but it's all I can manage.

"Feels like home," he says.

I extend my hand to him. "Guess we should properly meet. My name's Otis."

"Just call me Joe."

I doubt that's his real name. I'll stick with Homeless Man.

"Can I offer you some food?" I ask. "I don't have anything ready, but I can cook it in the shop. You like chicken?"

He doesn't smile, but he looks moved. "I would love that. Thank you, thank you."

I give a nod and return to the shop. I'm still nauseous, but at least it's dry in here. I take a breast out of the teriyaki marinade, throw it on the small George Foreman grill and let it simmer for seven minutes.

During those seven minutes, I still feel sick to my stomach, but I smile. I've been looking for ways to engage those around me, and the opportunity has been right in front of me for years. Even if it means one less sold piece of meat each week, it's a good deed performed. I'll even buy it with my own money so that it won't upset Andre's plan.

I kept my quarters to myself, but shared my food. I think I just created a new tradition.

12

It's early January. I'm outside. It's Dark. Foggy. Cold.
I'm not sure if you remember, but I'm on the verge of
arthritis, and being outside on a cold January night is not
conducive to my joints.

But that's the reason I'm out. I'm going to my doctor's
appointment. I don't love the idea of medicating my
pain, but I need something. I'm still a few years away
from retirement, and I need to keep my business
running. I can't afford to do otherwise.

My doctor's office is over in the West End, a ritzy
neighbourhood which I rarely frequent. The bus stops
about three blocks from the office. It's only six, but
darkness has long since fallen. I can't see much other
than what's lit by the street lamps, and there aren't many
sounds either.

Apart from a man's voice. It sounds like he's far away
and I can't quite make out the words, so I walk a little
further and listen. I make sure I'm out of sight and peer
around the corner of the building. I know this voice. I
just can't put a face to it.

I now can tell that two men are speaking. Shouting.

"What the hell is so complicated about getting your garbage in the can?"

"I'm sorry, sir, it was an honest mistake."

"I don't give a shit about an honest mistake. I want you to clean up after yourself."

"I will do my best, I don't mean to upset you, I never do."

"Then stop being lazy. Do you hear me? You're disgusting, and lazy, and this is pathetic. Have some decency!"

I hear footsteps. One of them must be leaving. I walk toward the source of the sound as it's on the way to my doctor. I hate gossip, I hate abuse, and I really don't need to know what's going on here, but curiosity has gotten the best of me tonight.

"Oh, sure, just walk away. Thanks for really making a change. Your lazy ass better not make a mess like this again."

I see a figure in the distance. It's the man who has been yelling the obscenities. I don't get too close, and I don't want to be obvious, but I glance over now to take a look. He's younger, in his early thirties, I assume at least as his back is toward me. There's an older man there as well, who I assume is the victim. No, I know he is. I just want to know who the younger man is. He starts to turn around, and I see his face as he turns back and heads inside his apartment.

I know who he is.

I know his face.

I know his name.

Will.

13

I'm back at Tim Hortons for lunch. I order the full chili combo with a medium coffee and an old fashion glazed donut, even though I don't have much of an appetite at the moment.

That's because I'm reading the newspaper. I know it's important to stay informed, but I honestly hate reading the news. There are horrific stories on every page, and I'm overwhelmed by sadness.

There is, however, one story that sticks out. It's about a man who gave away every bit of his money and possessions to his friends after he died. He had no family, but he loved many. He lived a humble life and secretly sat on a fortune. The friends were all interviewed after the will became public. None of them knew he had any such resources, and he never was one to brag. So they were grieved by his passing but blessed by his fearless generosity.

I don't have any family either, and the only thing I possess is my business. I do like the idea of serving others upon passing. It's inspiring. I hope I don't have to think of my death bed for quite some time, but I want to create a legacy. I have no idea what I could leave. Our desolate world needs more good news, though, and I'm so thankful for this man's story.

Now I can actually enjoy my lunch.

14

The bell on the shop's door just rang. I look up to see
Marla. I feel my heart become warm.

"Good afternoon, Otis," she says with a smile, holding
the door open but not coming inside.

"Hi, Marla."

"Well, turns out UGM doesn't need any donations for
the Easter dinner, but they're thankful for the offer.
Anyways, just wanted to give you an update."

"You're off already? Where to?"

"The library," she says. "More to learn."

"I feel like you live there!" I say." It's so beautiful
outside. Why not go for a walk around the park?"

"As long as there are no mountains in sight, then I'll
go," she says with a laugh. "Honestly, there's not
enough time in the day to think about myself."

"I would hardly call it selfish to take a walk," I say with a chuckle.

Her expression becomes heavy.

She steps inside and closes the door. "Have you seen this city? People describe it as a world-class destination, 'the most liveable city on Earth.' But you just walk a couple blocks away from Prada and Gucci and you're at the threshold of Hell. If I can bring some respite to someone today, or learn how to offer some relief to their pain, or even just remind them of their dignity, I'll be able to sleep tonight."

Marla makes her very existence a contribution to humanity.

"You give too much, Marla," I say.

She gives a pained smile. "You could say I'm paying off my debt." With that, she waves goodbye and opens the door to leave.

What a heavy burden she carries. Poor Marla.

15

I'm so used to things as I have come to know them. I know that Antonio will brew my coffee. I know that Kuldeep will give me my newspaper. I know that my food supplier will stock my inventory. I know that the lights will come on when I flip the switch. And even though it rains so often, I know that Vancouver is breathtaking when the sun appears. When things are different than how I've come to expect, I don't know how to handle them.

That's why I don't know how to interpret Sheila's behaviour today.

When she stormed into the shop, I almost didn't notice the difference. She wore a a purple Lululemon sweatshirt and grey yoga pants. Her hair, though, was tangled and down, not up and tidy. Her face was free of make-up, showing dark circles under her eyes. She looked tired. Frantic. Scattered.

"People are useless," she said as she marched up to the counter, nearly bumping into an elderly couple looking in the display case and digging in her purse for her phone. She always carries her phone in her hand; not today. "My hairstylist cancelled my appointment today. Whole day is thrown off now."

It sounded a bit dramatic, but I decided not to push it. Even though Sheila can be abrupt, it wasn't like her to be this abrasive. This unorganized.

"I need two salmon, clean and cut into steaks," she demanded.

I look down and see that there are only two steaks left in the display. She looks down at the same time and I can almost see a warning in her eyes when our gazes meet, telling me that it won't be in my best interest if those are all that remain.

"Tell me there are more in the back, Otis."

"I'm sorry, Sheila."

She slams her hand onto the glass, causing me and my other customers to jolt. "What the hell, Otis! When will you have more?"

I swallow before speaking, realizing my mouth has gone dry.

"My next shipment doesn't come until tomorrow," I finally say.

She glares at me, grabs her purse and storms out.

I look at the elderly couple, telling them that this isn't like Sheila.

Or is it? She spends so much time managing schedules, appearances and family members. What I saw wasn't glamorous, assured or controlled. For such a fierce determination to maintain her dominion, something had come unhinged. Maybe Sheila was just having a rough day.

Maybe later she regained some sense of normalcy after storming out of my shop.

Or, maybe I had seen the real Sheila for the first time today.

16

It's 5:30 on Thursday. Most of the working class have started to head home from their duties, which means that Andre should walk through the shop's door at any minute.

Andre comes every Thursday night for a sixteen-ounce cut of steak. Most people buy their luxury meats for Friday nights or the weekends, but Andre has a different schedule. He picks up a different girl every Friday night from a club, brings her home to his pristine condo and then sends her away after breakfast - always assuring her that he will call, but with no intention of ever following through. He once told me that he never brings her to the master bedroom, just the guest room, something about how it would send the wrong signal.

In order to keep up appearances, he cleans his condo from top to bottom, spending several hours of Thursday night doing so and then winding down with his steak and a bottle of Malbec.

I really didn't enjoy hearing this disclosure when he told me several years ago; I almost felt violated on behalf of these girls. But I listened. That's what I'm here for, and I've continued listening ever since. Part of that listening is having his steak ready for him when he walks in the door.

I'm working on inventory and preparing my next order while I wait.

Andre now walks through the door, dressed in his sharp business suit. He takes off his sunglasses as he gets to the counter, finishing off a text message. He puts his phone in his pocket with one hand and pulls out his wallet with his other hand, finally making eye contact as he hands over his credit card.

"Thursday night?" I ask, forcing a smile to mask my discomfort as I reach for his card.

Andre grins. He knows that I remember his rituals.

"Thursday night," he responds.

I process his payment, give him his receipt and then open the cooler to grab the pre-wrapped cut and place it in a plastic bag.

We nod to each other, and he is off.

I then go back to inventory, noting how much I still have in the cooler of each type of meat and then ordering accordingly. In some ways, I'm a planner just like Andre, but I plan out of need, not want. People should know their difference, like how to make the world a better place through their plans and actions. Why can't

Andre see that his desires and wants only benefit him and no one else? Maybe he'll understand it. One day he will.

I need to think of something pure, something better. Something noble to clean the air in the shop. I decide to cook up a steak for Homeless Man.

17

It's the second Wednesday of the month. There's nothing peculiar about this recurrence to me, but there is to Sheila. It's the day she gets her hair and nails done each month. The last time I saw her, her hairstylist had to cancel at the last minute. You remember, you were there as well.

I hardly even hear her when she walks in today. Her hair looks neither prim nor proper, her eyes hidden by the large sunglasses. She doesn't have her phone in her hand, and her shoulders are down.

"Good morning, Sheila," I finally say.

She takes off her sunglasses. Her eyes are red, swollen, free of any make-up. She looks at me for several seconds before speaking.

"Six chicken breasts," she says, her voice low and distant.

"How is your day going?" I ask, not even considering asking if she has a hair appointment today.
"Fast, as always. Truth is, I'd rather be at a bar, but I don't have time for that."

She pulls out her cheque book and a pen and looks down at the paper, not clicking the pen at all. She looks so tired. I haven't gotten her order together yet because I can tell something is wrong.

"I wish I had time," she says under her breath.

"Do you want to sit for a minute?" I ask, bringing out a folding chair from behind the counter. "Take a little break, Sheila, please."

She puts her cheque back in her purse and moves to the chair.

"I'm sorry I lost it on you, Otis," Sheila says. "You did nothing to deserve that. It just wasn't my day. I'm so good at maintaining a schedule, and it all just went to hell that day."

I've never known Sheila to let down her guard. I decide to encourage her to go further.

"You're used to a bit more control, I take it?" I ask.

She lets out a tired laugh.

"You could say that. Making up for a lot of chaos."

I don't say anything. People don't know how to sit in silence and will do anything they can to fill it. I stay quiet and let Sheila find her way out of the silence.

"Did you know I'm an American?" she eventually says.

"I didn't know that, no. Where from?"

"Sacramento, California. My family immigrated to Canada when I was young. Dad got a job in the oil fields. Paid really well. The price was living in Northern Alberta."

"Not a fan of the area, then?" I ask.

"None of us were. My mom never really wanted to be there, and my dad worked such crazy long hours that they rarely saw each other. She started spending time online. Remember ICQ? The early chat rooms, super taboo. Anyways, she started chatting with a guy, stayed up late in the night, talking about all kinds of deep personal stuff. She didn't play with us kids at all. Turned out to be a woman playing a nasty prank. 'Catfish,' they call it these days. Mom already hated life and that was her one escape, so she told us to go play in the yard while she went into the garage with the car engine running. She sat in the driver's seat with the window down. My little brother found her a couple hours later."

She paused for a moment. I feel sick to my stomach, but I don't say anything. I want to know the rest of the story. It's like she's talking to herself. I don't think she even knows I'm still here.

"Dad didn't know what to do," she continued. "Didn't know anything about being a father, stopped going to work, lost his job, fell into deep depression. Social services put each of us kids in different foster homes. I haven't seen them since I was eight."

"You've never seen them? Do you know where they are?"

"Don't know, don't care. As far as anyone is concerned, my parents died in a car crash and I'm an only child. That's the story everyone got. Once I moved to Vancouver and met my husband, we fell in love. I told him that story. He believed it. I made myself believe it, too. We got married, I was pregnant within the first year, and it became my life's work to protect my family from experiencing even a hint of the shit I went through."

She pauses again.

"That's why I just lose it when things don't go according to plan." Her voice is weak, but determined. "I *always* have a plan."

I finally find words to say, simple as they are.

"I'm so sorry, Sheila."

She looks at me, as if she just realized what she has told me. Her softness has gone, and some strength has returned to her eyes.

"This goes to the grave with you, Otis. I've never told anyone."

"I don't know how long I'll be around," I say, "but it's not my story to tell."

She stands up, pulls out her cheque book and pen again, clicking it twice. She then smiles a sincere smile of gratitude, which shines through her tired eyes.

"Well, how about those chicken breasts?" she says.

"Yes, about those," I respond.

I gather her order and place the wrapped cuts in a bag. I tell her the total and she writes me a cheque.
"What gets me most is that my kids just don't get how much I slave over this family, to protect them and keep them safe," she says, as if the conversation never stopped. "I always took such pride in how different I am from my parents, how present and engaged I am. Nothing's as devastating as realizing how different your kids are from you, and how much they *want* to be different from you. Maybe they'll get it someday, maybe they'll thank me. Just gotta keep them safe."

"Wouldn't they be more grateful if they knew your background?" I ask.

"Not an option, not an option. This is the story they get. Everyone's better off this way."

She puts her pen and cheque book back in her purse, takes the meat and is ready to go.

"Everyone's better off this way, Otis," she repeats. "I just have to keep the story straight."

18

It's Easter Sunday, which means I'm back at church.
Will's church, to be precise. Nearly every seat is filled. I
wonder how many are visitors like myself.

It's good to see so many people here. Christmas often
gets the most attention when it comes to religious
holidays - the birth of Christ, the Saviour of the world.
Even those outside the church doors understand that
day's significance.

Easter, on the other hand, is often reduced to chocolates
and bunnies, whereas it's equally significant when it
comes to religious implications: the Son of God dying a
humiliating death for the sake of all humanity; the hope
of salvation and redemption; the ultimate personification
of grace.

Will's sermon is focused on this very message.
Everyone here either believes in grace and redemption,
or they came here in search of this grace they so badly

need and want. Either way, everyone is listening intently.

I'm trying to listen, but I'm distracted. I can't look at Will or hear him preach without thinking back to that night. Besides the elderly man, I must be the only one in this building who knows that other side of Will.

How can Will be so loving and gracious and giving of his time, but so inhumane to his neighbour? Didn't Jesus say to love thy neighbour as thyself? Where is Will's love for that poor man?

I notice that Will occasionally looks to his left, then his eyes almost flinch shut as he turns back to the crowd. I finally follow his gaze, and I see that there's a mirror in the foyer visible from the stage.

He can't even look at his own reflection.

Could it be that Will doesn't even love himself? Is that why he treated his neighbour with such cruelty, because he's so cruel to himself? Does he force that gracious smile to mask his misery? If that's the case . . . I don't even know what to think. Other than that my heart truly breaks for Will. Why can't he see himself as his loving God sees him? If he could see that, surely he would then be able to love his neighbour more fully.

I decide to start listening to the sermon. Maybe I'll find some way I can help.

19

I knew this was going to be a rough day when I saw Marla crying on the sidewalk.

Other people walked around her, unsure how to respond to her tears.

I didn't approach her right away. I didn't know how to. This is Marla, happy, joyful, optimistic Marla, an angel on this side of heaven if there ever was one. And here she is, crying, sad, heartbroken, in agony. What was I to say?

I decide to say nothing. I walk up and sit down beside her instead. She doesn't look up, but she knows it's me. She leans against my shoulder. We sit in silence for several minutes.

"A patient died on my watch," she finally says Marla dedicates her life to her patients, and one of those lives was lost. That explains why it hit her so hard.

"What happened?" I ask.

She lets out a sob and struggles to catch her breath. Maybe I shouldn't have asked what happened.

"Mismanagement of medication," she says. "My mismanagement. I gave the wrong meds. Turns out she was allergic and went into anaphylactic shock. I couldn't revive her."

I can't think of any consolation, and I don't try to give any, because sometimes words just can't console. I hesitate, then I put my arm around her.

"I'm so sorry, Marla," is all I can say. "I can't imagine how hard this must be for you. I know how deeply you love your patients."

"This isn't supposed to happen," she says, sounding bitter. "I've read all the books. I've researched all the studies. I soared through nursing school. I . . . ."

She pauses.

"I wasn't going to let it happen again."

This time, I have no choice but to prod.

"Let what happen?"

She turns away and closes her eyes, tears seeping through and running down her cheeks.

"This isn't the first time I've killed someone."

I must have heard something wrong, or she just chose the wrong words. She must have meant that someone had died on her watch before.

"Did something similar happen with a patient?" I ask, waiting for her to clarify.

"It wasn't similar, and it wasn't a patient."

I don't say anything. I wait for her to continue. She props her arms on her knees, stares out in front of her and lets out a laugh that sounds more like defeat than joy.

"I'm a twin. Was a twin, rather. Maria." She pauses. "Beautiful, smart, wonderful Maria. Always excelled at everything when we were younger, and she always let me know."

"Was she a nurse too?" I ask.

"Might have been, if she made it past sixteen."

"She died when she was sixteen?"

"I couldn't take it anymore," she continued, ignoring my question. "Always second best, always watching from the sidelines. Never equal."

I again sit in silence, unsure where this is going. Her eyes harden.

"Me and Maria, we really hated each other. Always bickering. The only way my parents could make us get along was to pile us into the car and drive for hours on Saturdays for family hikes, far away from the city. Once we were out of our familiar area, we were fine. No idea why, but it always worked. But for all Maria's beauty, strength and wit, she had one weakness. A peanut allergy. And she had to carry an epi-pen with her at all times on a small fanny pack. She rarely ever had to use it, but always had the pack with her."

She pauses again, sniffs and wipes her nose with her sleeve. I want to offer her some of the hand sanitizer in my pocket, but I don't think it's the right time for that. Instead, I wait for the rest of the story.

"We were sixteen when it happened. We were fighting over something, I can't even remember what. She called me an ugly, nasty bitch. I don't know why, but at sixteen, those words cut me deeper than I could have imagined. And then . . ."

I re-adjust as the sidewalk is quite uncomfortable. Marla's eyes soften again, but she doesn't cry. I don't think she has any tears left.

"I told her that we shouldn't be fighting like this anymore, that we should take a drive together and do the only thing that ever got us to stop fighting: a hike. She shrugged, then she agreed. While she was in the bathroom, I went to her pack, and I took the pen out. I hid it in her top dresser drawer. She never opened the pack 'cause she never needed it, so she had no reason to check. When she came out, I had everything ready - our water, our sunscreen and some snacks. She just didn't know that I tucked a bag of peanuts in my pocket that I'd kept under my bed for years, waiting for the right moment to use them."

I suddenly feel sick. This has to be a dream, I tell myself. This isn't Marla. It can't be. I didn't even realize that I had slightly moved away from her.

"We were so far away from the hospital and out of cell service when I opened the bag. I threw the peanuts into a creek after she got exposed. When she reached for her epi-pen and saw it wasn't there, she realized what I had done. I just looked at her, not with any hate or animosity, but pity. Pity because the strong, fierce, untouchable Maria couldn't breathe, couldn't fight back, couldn't do anything. She knew who the stronger one was now." She stops for a few seconds, shoulders dropping. "And then she was gone."

Silence again. The tears stopped, but her eyes look so fatigued. So hollow. So unlike the Marla I know.

"I ran down the mountain and called an ambulance, already knowing it was too late, faking a sense of panic and hysterics. And the reality of what I did kicked in while I waited for help. While I stood by her body. I was crushed by the guilt of it all, sickened with what I'd become. What I *did*. Hell, I killed my *sister*. God, I hated her, but my *sister*."

That's why Marla can't look at mountains, I realize. I still don't say anything, but I pull my arm way.

"My parents divorced within the year, thinking it all was a tragic accident that God allowed. They had no idea it was my fault. So I suffered in silence and went into nursing school, swearing on Maria's life that I would make things right and that no one else would ever die at my hand. That I would prolong life, not cause any more death."

She pauses.

"And yet, here we are today," she says, dropping her head into her hands, sobbing again. I put my hand back on her shoulder, unsure of what else to do.

Through her tears, she whispers, "I'm so sorry, Maria."

20

I'm sitting at the Tim Hortons across the street from the shop, staring down at the chili I ordered almost an hour ago. What I see in front of me are beans, beef and mushrooms, sitting together in a disposable cup. The only thing that has changed since I ordered it is that the grease has started to collect at the surface; streaks of red liquid make their way to the edge of the bowl and up the side. I imagine it's quite cold now.

That doesn't matter, because while I've been looking at food, the only thoughts registering in my mind are those that concern Will, Sheila, Garret, Marla and Andre.

All I sought out to do was provide my customers with the best quality meat I could source, and I take so much pride in what has become my life's work. It has given me a tangible way to serve humanity. I have found my purpose.

And then these five people happened to me. I have been burdened by their confessions, and by what I've observed. Maybe they disclosed to me because, for some reason, I earned their trust? All I ever did was listen, which I thought was just a common courtesy. Yet I've gone from being their butcher to their priest, only with qualifications for the former.

The thing is, I didn't ask for any of this. I didn't seek out their tragic stories in hopes of redeeming them. Even if I did, how could I? I'm just a member of the working class on his way to retirement.

But what if I'm not finished with my work? What if I'm meant to help these five souls? What if I can find some way to speak truth into their lives, to help them turn from their ways, to inspire them to live a better story than the tales they've been telling? I don't even know where'd I'd start, though.

I decide to eat my cold chili instead.

21

I have my copy of the *Vancouver Sun* on the counter and opened up to the story, my coffee still warm. Daily newspapers don't have much shelf life, but there's a story in this issue that has people's attention.

You remember Homeless Man, the gentleman who has resided near my shop for years. We had become acquainted over the last several months as I gave him warm meals. I found out he used to be an elementary teacher who was married to his high school sweetheart. They were driving home from a date one evening and got in a car accident caused by a drunk driver. Homeless Man survived, she didn't.

He was a wonderful man who had experienced tragedies of his own, and who was taken down a road of destitution which led him to this alley.

However, he passed away a few days ago from what looked like an overdose, right at the edge of the sidewalk outside my shop. I was heartbroken to find him there when I came to work that morning.

I called the police to report the incident, and I shared how I had come to know him. How he had so much potential but was dealt some harsh cards, and how I truly thought he desired to get better and turn his life back around.

I told all of this to the police, as well as that I was going to have a donation jar in my shop for people to contribute toward local shelters and rehabilitation centres, services that I believe would have helped reshape the fate of this man, my friend.

A reporter for the newspaper heard about this somehow, and she came and interviewed me about Homeless Man and the donation jar. I was a little nervous to be featured as I didn't want any attention on myself, but I also knew it would help share this tragic outcome and bring attention to all the amazing services available in the city.

And you know what? Lots of people have come by to donate. Most of them are new faces, and not many of them bought meat while they were in, but that was never the goal. More than anything, I was thrilled to see Will, Sheila, Garret, Marla and Andre all come in. They bought their usual purchases and also gave generous donations. Here's the moving part: each of them told me that Homeless Man's story made an impact on them, that they were shaken, unsettled by how no one ever plans to end up where they are, and that this tragedy had inspired them to really examine their own lives.

They told me themselves that it caused them to look inward. I sincerely believe that this will bring about change in their lives.

That Sheila will surrender her reign of control and let her family in.

That Will can extend God's unconditional love to himself and thus to his neighbour as well.

That Andre might discover meaningful human connection and seek out his forgotten family.

That Marla can forgive herself for her sins and find rest for her tortured soul.

That Garret will lose his thirst for the spotlight and lead his revolution in peace rather than violence or self-glorification.

I am still so deeply moved by this. I pray that their self-examinations lead them to healing, to redemption, to peace.

It seems that there is hope for them after all.

22

When we first met, I told you that my name is Otis.
Now, I'll tell you something else: I have a secret, too.

The story of Homeless Man being a widowed teacher? I
made that up.

Convincing, wasn't it?

Also, I know that Homeless Man didn't die of an
overdose. I know this because I did it.

It all happened through our usual exchange, nothing out
of the ordinary that would raise suspicion. It wasn't even
that drastic of a move. I didn't strangle him or hire
someone to take him out. All I did was give him a cut of
steak drenched in teriyaki sauce mixed with a generous
serving of arsenic. No autopsy or investigation was
performed, so my secret literally went to the grave with
him.

I had no choice, really. Did you honestly think that
Sheila, Will, Andre, Marla or Garret would have bettered
their stories if I didn't somehow intervene? They're all

off to re-write their destinies now. They'd better be. It took death to wake them up.

The thing is, that meal gave Homeless Man a different story. He no longer was an invisible person on the side of the street; he now will be remembered as a real, breathing human being who could have known a far better reality. That's the story everyone gets, at least.

We are all part of a big mess, and often it requires something drastic to clean up that mess and transform it back into beauty.

Maybe I am deranged, but is that really so unusual?

So rare?

Am I that different from them?

Or even from you?

I may be nearing retirement, but clearly I have more work to do in this world. Never underestimate the power of a good story and a captive audience. I convinced you, after all.

Well, it's that time of the morning again. I switch the sign to "Open," unlock the door and wait for the first customer to arrive.

Charades

ABOUT THE AUTHOR

Todd Foley is an American who made the move to British Columbia, Canada, where he lives with his wife and growing family. He is the author or *Eastbound Sailing* and *Man Speak*. He finds inspiration for storytelling via his unorganized bookshelf, a non-sequiter Netflix queue and using public transit.

Made in the USA
San Bernardino, CA
17 August 2016